ROARING

Whisper

Story by
Gabriel Bench

Illustrations by
Pete Berg

Printed in the U.S.A.

Library of Congress Control Number 2011900921
ISBN #978-1453728154

Published by:
Humble Bee Books
PMB A-3 • 621 SR 9 NE • Lake Stevens WA 98258

Roaring Whisper: An entertaining story about the importance of taking time to listen to the Most High King.

Other books include:

Ester Bunny: released December 2008. A heartwarming and inspiring folk tale about overcoming obstacles and reaching for one's dreams.

Evan Bunny: released July 2009. Sequel to Ester Bunny. A winning story about pride, humility and second chances.

Ella Bunny: released December 2009 A story for children. A message for all about the power of love.

To view previews you may visit www.humblebeebooks.com

ROARING

Whisper

Dedicated to the Holy Spirit and to my first granddaughter, Melody.
Big thanks to Jeff Bench for editing the story
and to Holly Zvonec for her insight.

A roaring thank you to Pete Berg for his continued anointed illustrations
that bring the stories to life.

And more than a thank you is needed for my wife Sandy
who daily prays with me and for me.

Upon all time there lives the Most High King.

From stories told, those who have caught a glimpse of Him describe the King as looking most like a mighty lion made of pure light.

Ever changing colors continually leap from the center of His being, radiating His power and love.

His paws alone shining as bright as stars. Some say the stars in the sky are His living paw prints.

How the Most High King talks to His subjects
is a mystery.

No one has ever seen Him open His mouth,
but His **ROAR** can surely be heard.

He knows the secrets of the universe, and when
He roars, sometimes His roars are heard as a whisper
and sometimes His whispers can be heard as a roar.

Can you imagine how the wind is connected to the color of a flower or how a book can be alive?

How about this: imagine how what you can see is less real than what you can't see.

The Most High King knows these mysteries and secrets and freely shares them.

Long ago when there was less noise in the universe,

the King's roars could easily be heard.

It is easier to explain in a story, so…

Once upon a time,
the roars of the Most High King communicated everything
the animals of the world needed to know to live peaceful,
healthy, joyous lives.

All of the animals made sure they took time every day to be still
and listen for His roars. His roars brought comfort,
revealed what foods to eat, where to travel, and many other helpful things.

The most mysterious and valuable part of the King's ROARS
revealed the wonders of the unseen. Not only the unseen
related to the here and now, like heat from the sun,
but the unseen that lasts forever.

The animals just called it,
"Roar Language".

One day, in a village, a dazzling elephant was born...
or should I say launched?...
announced?... propelled?...

oh my, well, let's just say he burst onto
the scene making very loud trumpeting sounds.

His trumpet sounds were so loud they blew the doctor right out of the hut.

Most unfortunate though,
because his trumpet sounds
were so loud,
this dazzling elephant did not hear
the Most High King's roaring whisper of love
like all the other newborns heard.

He was named Bugle,
and Bugle liked blowing his horn
all of the time.

Bugle loved to blow his horn so much
that he did not take the time to learn Roar Language.

One time, Gerry the Giraffe and Alan the Aardvark
talked to Bugle about Roar Language,
and Bugle got very upset.

Bugle filled his lungs as large as a hot air balloon,
then he blew a trumpet blast so strong
it blew all the fur right off of Alan.

This did not stop Alan,
but after that,
no other animal dared to say anything
to Bugle about Roar Language.

During his youth and young adult years
Bugle crafted his horn blowing
into beautiful sounds with a captivating beat.

Bugle grew to be the largest elephant
in any herd for miles and miles.

And remember,
since Bugle did not know Roar Language,
he did not learn any of the Most High King's secrets.

He had never seen this king
and he didn't believe in anything
he couldn't see with his own eyes.

Being so large,
   Bugle knew other animals looked up to him
                  in more ways than one.

                     He also knew his horn blowing
                  had magical effects on the other animals,
               especially the younger ones.

      They enjoyed listening to his upbeat music so much
that they stopped taking time to listen for Roar Language.

         Over time,
      they wondered if Roar Language was even real.

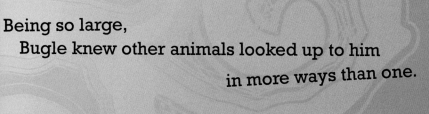

hen he was not playing music,

Bugle shared his thoughts about life.

Because Bugle did not know or care about Roar Language
his thoughts lacked wisdom or truth.

The other animals thought,
since Bugle played such beautiful music,
he must be right about everything,
but they were wrong.

As time went on,
more and more animals in the area
stopped paying attention to the roars
and started paying more attention
to Bugle's music and beliefs.

They were so taken in by Bugle
that they asked Bugle to be the king
over all of the villages in the area.

Bugle gladly accepted.

King Bugle soon grew tired of hearing how
the "roar people" disagreed
with what he wanted,
so he banned Roar Language.

He declared,
"Anyone found speaking about Roar Language
or the unseen Roar King
will be sent out of my kingdom."

Alan the Aardvark led a group of banished animals
on a long journey
to Twin Town,
where they were happy
to find Roar Language
alive and well.

After Bugle grew very old,
his long reign as king finally came to a close.

He turned his kingdom over to his son,
Bugle Junior.
By this time, Roar Language
had been forgotten in the Bugle kingdom.

The Bugle kingdom expanded,
but food became harder to find.
What was once a land filled with
lush green plants and fruit
had slowly been changing,
leaving nothing but dusty brown dirt.

Bugle Junior did not know,
but when the last animal that understood Roar Language was gone,
the source of keeping the plants healthy
and growing enough food also left with him.

Hungry animals
can get mean,
so Bugle Junior decided
to take his best scouts on a trip
to find a new source of food.

They wandered into a new area
filled with many plant forms.
Bugle Junior saw some tall bright green plants
dripping with sweet smelling,
plum-sized berries flowing from the stems.

Bugle Junior's mouth watered
as he announced,
"Here is our new food source!"

The scouts rushed around
digging up all of the berry plants
they could find to bring home.

he animals cheered
as Bugle Junior and the scouting party
returned with the bright
and juicy looking
food plants.

A great feast was held
and many berries were eaten.
Bugle Junior was blowing his horn
in a soothing rhythm
as many animals danced
around the crackling fire.

They danced and
sang praises
to Bugle Junior
well into the evening.

Zander Zebra was
the last animal
to give a big yawn
and doze off
to sleep
as the last
orange embers of the
once mighty fire
winked goodnight.

 heavy mist was floating in the morning air,
but instead of hearing the usual chirps of birds,
all that could be heard
was awful groans.

Many of the animals were sick
and no one knew what to do.

Finally, Topper Toucan popped up squawking,
"I have an idea."
He said he had a cousin, Toby Toucan,
who was a doctor
living in the not-so-liked Twin Town,
who might be able to help.

Bugle Junior weakly pulled himself up and said, "Send for the doctor."

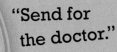

Twin Town was a long way away,
but Toby Toucan and his nurse, Melody Macaw,
made it back to the Bugle kingdom
as fast as they could fly.

Toby used his usual methods to find out what was causing the sickness
and what was needed to heal the animals.
He would hop a bit, squawk a bit, flit a bit,
cock his head and beak left, then right,
then back left again.
Looking puzzled, he tried again,
hopping, squawking, flitting
and cocking his head.

Finally, Toby squawked,
"I don't know why the animals are sick.
With all of the noise in the air
I can't hear the King's roar."

A hush fell over the area
as every animal looked at Bugle Junior
to see what he would do.

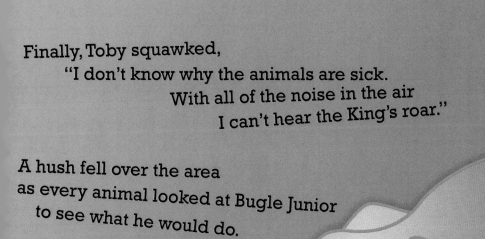

Bugle Junior
was too weak
to protest.

Melody Macaw was gifted at hearing
and understanding Roar Language,
but like Toby,
she was only hearing noise.

She cooed and cawed
and then said,
"The noise is coming from right here
in the Bugle kingdom."

Melody humbly suggested
they hold a day of silence and prayer
to the Most High King
to see if it would help them
to hear His roar.

oby agreed and delivered this message
to King Bugle Junior.

Bugle Junior said,
"Enough of this foolishness.
We will get a real doctor to help us."

All of the local doctors were called in,
but none of them could cure the sickness.

Finally, many of the animals took courage
and begged Bugle Junior to allow

the day of silence and prayer.

Fearing he would die,
and seeing no other options,
Bugle Junior agreed.

All of the animals that could move
gathered for the day of silence and prayer.
Toby led the prayer
as Melody gracefully flew over the area,
cooing and cawing.
Suddenly, the weather started to change.
Dark clouds appeared, blocking out the sun.
Then came pounding rain.
To the untrained ear,
the rain only confirmed the prayers were not working,
but to Melody,
the sound of each raindrop falling
shouted out the roars of the Most High King.

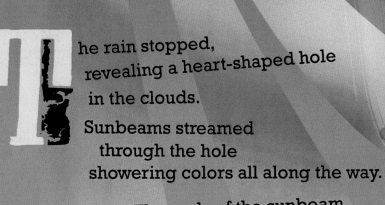

The rain stopped,
revealing a heart-shaped hole
in the clouds.

Sunbeams streamed
through the hole
showering colors all along the way.

The ends of the sunbeam
looked like colorful glowing hands
racing to cradle a small pond
where pink lilies were rocking
back and forth on shimmering water.

The Most High King's roar
embraced Melody.
She then understood
what was causing the sickness
and what was needed to heal the animals.

She and Toby quickly began mixing pink lilies
with other ingredients
to form a pinkish-brown paste
they gave to all of the sick animals,
starting with King Bugle Junior.

The sick animals
recovered immediately.

When King Bugle Junior
thanked Melody and Toby
for saving his life,
Melody said "Don't thank us,
thank the Most High King,
because it was His loving roar
that showed us what to do."

Afterwards,
King Bugle Junior allowed
Roar Language
back into his kingdom
and invited a group from Twin Town
led by Andrea Aardvark,
to come and teach the animals
how to hear
Roar Language.

As the animals of Bugle kingdom learned Roar Language and to apply its truths, over time the dry, dusty brown dirt returned to being covered with healthy green plant life.

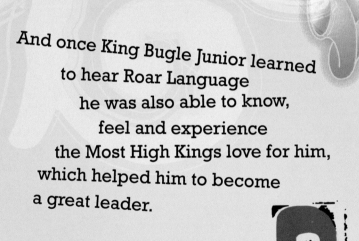

And once King Bugle Junior learned
to hear Roar Language
he was also able to know,
feel and experience
the Most High Kings love for him,
which helped him to become
a great leader.

So remember,
the Most High King loves you
and speaks exactly
what you need every day.
If you take the time to block out the noise
and listen for His roars
you will be able to hear them.
Sometimes as a **ROAR**
and sometimes as a *whisper*...

PARENT/TEACHER GUIDE

QUESTIONS TO ASK YOUR CHILD/CHILDREN OR STUDENTS:

The story gives examples of the Most High King's mysteries, one of them being a book that is living. Do you think this is possible? Can you think of a book that is living?

Do you believe Roar Language is real? If you do, what do you think would help you to learn and hear Roar Language?

King Bugle and King Bugle Junior did not take the time to learn Roar Language and even spoke against it. What happened as a result?

In the story, when the day of prayer and silence began, dark clouds formed in the sky and it started to rain. All the animals thought this was a bad thing, but was it? Why?

If the Most High King of the universe knew everything about everything, loved you, and wanted the best for you, would you want to spend time with Him? Would you want to be able to hear what he had to say to you? Why?

What things do you allow to get in the way of spending quiet time with the Most High King?

Do you have a time set aside where you cut out all of the noise (TV, video games, computer, music, cell phone, activities, etc.) so you can pray and listen for His voice? If not, when would be a good time to set aside for this activity?

Made in the USA
Columbia, SC
28 November 2022

71908643R00018